FUTURE SPY

FUTURE SPY

by

William J. Logan Jr.

iUniverse, Inc.
New York   Bloomington

Future Spy

*This is a work of fiction. All of the characters, names, incidents,
organizations, and dialogue in this novel are either the products
of the author's imagination or are used fictitiously.*

iUniverse books may be ordered through booksellers or by contacting:

iUniverse
1663 Liberty Drive
Bloomington, IN 47403
www.iuniverse.com
1-800-Authors (1-800-288-4677)

ISBN: 978-1-4401-4508-7 (pbk)
ISBN: 978-1-4401-4509-4 (dj)
ISBN: 978-1-4401-4507-0 (ebk)

Printed in the United States of America

iUniverse rev. date: 5/18/2009

This novel is dedicated my wife Pat who always
believed in me and the 'Twelfth of Never'

.

Thank you to Bonnie and Gail and my brother Philip.
Special thanks to Susan Aikman.

PROLOGUE

"What do we have nurse?" said Doctor Webb at Quantico Marine Base Hospital.

"The patient, a Mr. Nagol, was shot in the chest while trying to escape. His BP is 90 over 55 and dropping fast," said the nurse.

"OK, alert surgery that we have a hot one coming and let's get him moving," said Dr. Webb. Minutes later Mr. Nagol was wheeled into surgery.

In an adjacent surgical room, a woman named Wendy was delivering her first child. The time was 7:30 AM, August 3, 1942; the exact date and time of death for Mr. Nagol. Those in the hallway outside the operating rooms were jolted by a series of screams they thought were coming from the delivery room. They were wrong. The screams were in fact coming from the doctors and nurses attending to Mr. Nagol's body. You see, at the time of his death, his body just disappeared from the operating table.

About the same time, in a specially built vault at Quantico, Virginia, agents of the FBI witnessed a flash of light and a number of top-secret items suddenly vanished.

My name is William Nagol and I was born on August 3, 1942. I retired on June 16, 2008. Oh, by the way, I was also arrested and imprisoned by the FBI as an American spy at age 67 in January 1942. Confused? The reader of this novel should remember the information about both Mr. Nagol's death and the birth of the child at the Quantico hospital. Within these two events lies the solution to this puzzling tale. I use the word tale because although everything I relate in this story is true, most readers will say it is just an interesting tale.

CHAPTER ONE

She was a beauty. She carried herself well as she glided by me and her scent was of a saltwater breeze. I was truly in love with her. If my wife had heard me I probably would have been accused of adultery. No, I was referring to the boat I was about to buy. She was a 1985 Bertram, 54 feet long, fiberglass, with twin diesels, tuna tower, outriggers and a fully restored interior. At $562,000, the delivery was free. After working for so many years as a police officer and for the Department of Homeland Security I was finally retiring and the boat was not only going to take me into retirement but with rentals, put extra money in my pocket. I even had a name for her; **Adventure**. I was going to name her after my wife but as I said adultery will get you divorced. Well, actually it was her boat and I was just the captain I had a hat and everything. The current owner had the boat brought up from Florida and it had just sailed past me at the

1

dock and was edging into her berth. I had brought along my old navy buddy Joe, to help go over her one last time before signing the final papers. I was being overcautious even though the insurance company had already signed off on her sea worthiness. I guess after all the trouble I had finding the boat and having sold the house to finance her, I just wanted reassurance that the boat wouldn't end up being a money pit. Of course, if I had known that the boat would shortly cause me to be arrested and almost killed by the FBI I would have stayed on shore.

CHAPTER TWO

"Please sign here and here. You understand that the first payment will be in 45 days and the loan can be paid off at anytime," said the bank manager.

My wife Pat and I had been at the bank for about an hour reading all the formal language of the loan. It wasn't much different than buying a car with the clerk leaving the cubicle several to talk to the manager when we asked about the interest rate and small print font on the documents. You would think that a bank would have more comfortable chairs and private offices as it appeared that everyone in the bank could hear what was being said. I was also sweating at the prospect of shelling out the amount of money equal to my past home mortgage for a boat bobbing at the dock. Was retirement really here? It seemed I was in high school just last month. I guess I was having second thoughts, but the fact that I had three children, four grandchildren and a social security check being deposited in my bank account reminded me of my age. So with a quick stroke of the pen, I was captain of our new floating home on the water.

"For a minute I thought you weren't going to sign the papers and leave me homeless in there. I was thinking of stealing a shopping cart to store my things. "That would never happen", I said. "Your shoes alone wouldn't fit is a shopping cart. " Very funny", said Pat and then the frown turned to laughter and she said, "Let's celebrate. There is a good restaurant around the corner and I'm starved," Pat said as she hugged my arm and steered me toward the restaurant. Of course it was one of the most expensive in town. My wife never and I mean never believed that one should go second class. As we entered the restaurant I wished that I had dressed better given the second look by the hostess and the words, " Well, would you follow me", but the waiter was polite. I guess a tip is a tip.

After ordering and waiting for what seemed like an hour for our meal to arrive and Pat reaching over to steal my pickle off of my plate, I asked if she was still bothered about me taking a solo shake down cruise out in the Atlantic before joining her in Miami. Pat stopped in mid-bite.

"Well maybe a little. I really wish you would reconsider and take me. I could be good company at night," Pat said with a laugh and nearly chocking on her sandwich. "But I guess the short distance from the coast and the fact that the Coast Guard will be keeping an eye on you helps even though lately, you seem to live at the hospital after falling off of the ladder and tripping in the garden. Seriously, you have been at the hospital so much lately they keep your records at the front desk."

I tried to reassure her that I had been sailing for years but she just stared at me holding her sandwich like a pointed finger. I knew what she was thinking. It was an old accusation. Pat always told me that since I am an identical twin I only got half a brain. I didn't say a word. Women!

CHAPTER THREE

It was the ninth of September in 2008, and the weather was perfect. The wasn't a cloud in the sky, the temperature was 82 degrees and swells were a comfortable two feet with just enough wind so I could feel and smell the waters mist.I had checked the weather service and the forecast promised good weather through Saturday when I was expected to return to Baltimore. My shake-down cruise would take me down the Chesapeake Bay and out into the Atlantic for three days. Pat mentioned that she used to watch Gilligan's Island and a lot can happen in three days. Pat was on the dock to see me off and I could see her rubbing her nose which was a clear sign that she was worried about the trip. I again reassured her that I had a sound ship and all instruments were working fine. I also reminded her that I alerted the Coast Guard of my course and I had ship to shore capabilities and I had my cell phone so she could call me.

"Oh, I'm not worried about you or the boat. I'm just worried about your DVD collection you stored on the boat. You love that collection and if it is lost at sea, I am not sure what you would do," said Pat.

" Ouch! Pat had needled me about stowing my four hundred or so DVDs on the boat. I had given the excuse that I might lose them if I placed them in storage. I loved my collection and had grand visions of me and my buddies sitting around on the boat and watching the movies. I gave her a final hug and kiss and castoff from the dock.

CHAPTER FOUR

I cleared the Bay Bridge and Patuxent Naval Air Station and marveled at the numerous islands that had almost disappeared due to the rise in the water level in the Bay. In a few years, they would completely disappear. Towards evening I reached the Atlantic and set a course south towards Norfolk, Virginia. There wasn't much traffic and I made sure that I kept clear of any large ships heading towards Baltimore. The boat was responding better that I had anticipated which started to make me feel better about the purchase price. I began to laugh as I remembered Pat telling me that if we didn't find a house soon I would be walking around a piano on the deck and she even paced off the stern deck to see if it would fit. She had a habit of not stating the obvious but seemed to always to get her point across after 40 years of marriage. All in all, she was a keeper.

CHAPTER FIVE

I should have slept more but the excitement of the boat and sailing alone had kept me at the wheel most of the night. My instruments showed me approximately seventy-five miles East of Norfolk, Virginia and I would be turning for home in about five hours. Radar showed no other craft in the area so I decided to retract sails and let the boat drift while I stretched out on the wheelhouse deck for a short nap. As I started to reduce sails, I turned around I noticed that the magnetic compass was spinning around and the sails had lost wind. In fact it felt that the boat had hit the brakes when she suddenly stopped dead in the water and the engine died. I tried to start the engine but the gauge showed no voltage. The radio and the GPS were also off-line. Then I saw it. It was a wall of white coming towards me from the bow at about a hundred yards away and moving fast. It wasn't fog or a cloud. There seemed to be a white sheet billowing out and driven by some unfelt wind. It was huge and seemed to go on forever. The white wall kept coming closer and closer until it had enveloped the entire boat. My head started spinning and everything started going black. I felt like I was falling in slow motion down some black tunnel and the boat seemed to swirl around me. I tried to grab onto something, anything but I kept falling. The last thing I remembered was a sudden pain on my forehead as I collapsed on the deck.

CHAPTER SIX

The USS Nicholson had been detached from Norfolk Virginia. Its present location was approximately seventy miles east of Norfolk and the crew was conducting the routine watch in the area. Lieutenant Wilson peered through his binoculars, slowly scanning the choppy seas in front of the Nicholson looking for the telltale feather of a periscope moving through the water. It was a cold, bright March morning which had dawned thirty minutes earlier. Visibility was limitless, perfect for detecting the white wake of a periscope or for someone peering through a periscope to see you. It was a long, tedious exercise of trying to spot the enemy before he could spot you and get into position to take a shot. Lieutenant Wilson, the Officer of the Deck and known to the crew as the OOD, and his bridge team had been on watch for a little over two hours and had another two to go. Although they were only seventy miles from Norfolk, and a much needed couple of weeks in the yards for repairs, he had warned the bridge team that they were still in very dangerous waters. German U-boats had been operating in these waters for some time, and many an unwary merchant vessel had been sent to the bottom upon meeting the U-boats.

His team was well aware of the dangers the Germans posed. They had just been detached from escorting a convoy of merchant vessels returning from England. Five of those vessels would never reach port because of torpedoes from a German U-boat group known as a Wolfpack. Lieutenant Wilson did not wish the Nicholson to be one of their next targets. Just after the Bosn of the Watch sounded five bells, meaning it was six thirty in the morning, the sound powered phone shouted out, "Officer of the Deck, radar reports possible surface contact bearing 340 relative, range 12 miles."

Lieutenant Wilson immediately brought his binoculars around to the relative bearing while calling out to his bridge wing lookouts to confirm the possible contact. No sooner had the command passed his lips when the Bosn sang out "Captain on the Bridge."

Commander Keating, the Nicholson's commanding officer, crossed to his chair and pulled his own binoculars from their case and calmly said "Report."

Lieutenant Wilson ran through the litany he had gone through many times before. "Sir, the Nicholson is currently seventy five miles north, northeast of Norfolk, heading 215, speed fifteen knots, radar reports possible surface contact bearing 340 relative, distance twelve miles, negative visual contact."

Commander Keating raised has glasses while uttering the perfunctory, "very well."

A few moments later Seaman Dominick called out "Visual contact 330 relative, white hull low on the water."

The Captain and the OOD moved their gazes a few degrees further left straining to see the same contact the sharp eyed teenager had reported. The radar operator confirmed the contact bearing and stated the radar return on the contact was much stronger and the contact was now at ten and a half miles. Commander Keating turned to the OOD and said "Mr. Wilson, bring us in close enough to get a look at that contact, but put us up sun. If it is Fritz out there I want them to be looking into the sun."

Lt. Wilson turned his head slightly and called out "Helm, left standard rudder, steady course one hundred and sixty." "Aye Sir, my rudder is left standard, coming to new course one hundred and sixty."

As the bow swung steadily left, the Captain and the OOD joined the starboard lookout on the bridge wing to continue to study the contact.

"I have a good visual, Sir," announced Seaman Dominick. "White civilian boat with a tuna tower and dual outriggers. I estimate fifty feet in length. Cannot locate anyone aboard. Might be adrift, Sir."

The helmsman reported steady on course one hundred eighty and the contact slowly started to slide down the ship's starboard beam while the range between the two vessels slowly decreased. Still peering through his binoculars and scanning the area for indications of a possible sub, Lieutenant Wilson nervously asked the Captain what he intended to do about the sail boat. He was almost certain this was a trap. Why else would such a small vessel be this far from land in waters known to be patrolled by U-boats. The Captain ran through their options very quickly.

"If the boat is a trap, it's best that the Nicholson deal with the vessel because of our anti-submarine capability. She can handle problems better than a lightly or unarmed vessel. If she is just a distressed vessel we will check for any injured or incapacitated individuals and have a skeleton crew sail her into Norfolk. If she is derelict we will sink her as a hazard to navigation." He then instructed Lieutenant Wilson to activate the ship's sonar. Sonar was a very useful tool when checking for submerge objects. An audible sound, or "ping" was transmitted into the water and would bounce off the submerged object and return to the sender. By knowing the speed of sound through the water you could determine the contacts range from you. By moving the receiver you could determine direction. The downside to using sonar was that you were putting sound into the water and anyone that was close enough to hear the pings would be alerted to your presence. As Nicholson closed to within one nautical mile of the boat, and with no contacts either on radar or sonar, the Captain had the OOD slow the ship to three knots and circle the vessel.

"Helm, indicate ahead one third make revolutions for three knots"

"Aye Sir, engine room acknowledges ahead one third making revolutions for three knots."

"Very well, right five degrees rudder."

"Aye Sir, my rudder is right five degrees, no heading given."

"Very Well," finished the ODD as he stepped to the port bridge wing at the same time the Captain began hailing the drifting vessel with a bull horn.

"Mr. Wilson, have the Chief Bosn organize a boarding party and get Lieutenant Junior Grade Johnson up here. We'll put him in charge of the party. Bring the ship around on her starboard lee so the current won't drive us down on her."

Mr. Wilson turned to the Messenger of the Watch and said, "Tell the Chief Bosn to prepare the starboard motor whale boat and pick a crew for a boarding party. Tell him that Mr. Johnson will be in charge. Then get Mr. Johnson up here so the Captain can brief him."

"Helm shift your rudder."

"Aye Sir, my rudder is left five degrees, no heading given."

"Very well, all engines stop."

"Aye Sir, engine room acknowledges all engines stop."

The combination of the left rudder and stopping the propellers rotation allowed the Nicholson's momentum to carry the big ship slightly less than half a mile down current of the sailboat.

Lieutenant Wilson ordered, "Rudder amidships."

The helmsman spun the ships wheel to bring the rudder to a neutral position and said "Aye Sir, rudder amidships."

"All engines, back one third."

"Aye Sir, engine acknowledges all engines back one third."

The Nicholson vibrated noticeably as the vessel overcame it's forward momentum and neared a full stop. Lieutenant Wilson ordered, "All engines stop." The Helm responded, "Aye Sir, engine room acknowledges all engines stop."

Just then Lieutenant Johnson entered the bridge. The Captain looked up and said, "Take the starboard motor whaleboat and check out that boat. If she's seaworthy stay aboard with one other sailor and bring her into Norfolk. If she's not seaworthy get back here and we'll sink her. As soon as you have assessed the situation, we'll get underway again so we're not just sitting ducks out here."

Lieutenant Johnson snapped a quick salute, barked, "Aye, Aye Sir" and headed aft towards the starboard boat davit.

"Mr. Wilson, as soon as they're clear get us back underway and continue to circle the boat and make sure the lookouts are alert."

After the motor whaleboat had been lowered, disconnected from the davit and started heading for the boat, the Nicholson again began its slow circle around the boat.

CHAPTER SEVEN

I don't know how long I was out but suddenly I was aware that I was being pulled upright by my arms. I could hear shouting and knew I was surrounded by people. As my eyes slowly focused, I saw a large grey wall in front of me and I was being dragged towards it. I was still dizzy and started to vomit which brought curses from my new found friends. I remember being dragged off my boat and up steps attached to the grey wall. Only at the top of the ladder did I realize that I was on a U.S. Naval ship, probably a destroyer. Again I vomited and was pushed through a doorway, down steps and finally thrown onto the floor of a small metal cell. The last thing I heard was the clanging of a cell door being closed before I lost conscious again.

I don't know how long I was out but when I awoke I was lying on a bunk, my clothes had been taken and I was dressed in what appeared to be medical scrubs.

My hand went to my head and I found a bandage on my right temple through which I could feel stitches. I tried to sit up and finally did once the room stopped spinning. The room was about fifty feet square in size. The walls were battleship grey and except for a toilet, sink and bunk that I was sitting on, it was devoid of all other furniture. Through the cell bars I could see what appeared to be a seaman with sidearm. I called out to him and asked if he knew why I was here but was met with stoic silence. My head began to swim again and I laid down on the bunk and fell asleep.

CHAPTER EIGHT

I don't know how much time had passed but I was awakened by the sound of the cell door being opened. Two armed seaman entered accompanied by what appeared to be a naval officer with the rank of lieutenant. The lieutenant identified himself as Mr. Hopper and asked me my name and nationality. I told him that I was an American who lived in Baltimore, Maryland and that I was on a shake down cruise for my new ship, the Adventurer.

The Lieutenant then said, "Sir, I don't know what you are pulling but you are being held as a spy and not subject to the Geneva Convention regarding Prisoners of War as you were apprehended in civilian clothes attempting to enter the United States. You will shortly be transferred to the Coast Guard and then to the Norfolk Naval Base to be turned over to the FBI."

The lieutenant turned and left and a sailor brought in some food. He and my armed guard then wordlessly left and locked the cell door behind them.

CHAPTER NINE

My head was spinning and not like before. Spy! No! This was some kind of joke. I had identification. The Adventurer was registered. I had filed my route with the Coast Guard. My mind was thinking a million things at once. What the hell was going on? I walked to the cell door and demanded that the guard call the Captain. No response. I then demanded my cell phone to call my wife and have her call my attorney. Again, no response. I started to pace my cell but finally sat on my bunk as I realized that neither talking nor pacing helped. Well, at least I hadn't been shot yet.

I must have dozed off because when I woke, the ship had quit moving. I heard some commotion in the hallway and then the door opened and several men in civilian clothes entered accompanied by Lieutenant Hopper and another person I took to be a officer. I knew the bars on his uniform meant he held the rank of commander. The commander talked briefly with the two men in suits and then left.

One of the suits approached the cell, looked at me briefly and said, " Sir, my name is Special Agent Tom Harmon and my partner over there is Special Agent Don Harris. We are with the FBI and will be escorting you to a base facility for questioning. I understand that you have been advised that you are being treated as a spy for the Japanese government and that you have no rights under the Geneva Convention. Before transporting you ashore, there are several questions I would like to ask. What is your name?"

"My name is William Nagol."

"What is your nationality?"

"American."

"Where and when were you born?"

"Virginia, 1942."

"Address in the United States?"

1527 Ascot Street, Baltimore, Maryland."

"Phone Number?"

"Area Code 401-555-9872."

"What is an area code?"

"What?"

"What do you mean by area code?"

"You know, the first part of your phone number that indicates what part of the country you live in."

"Are you trying to be funny?"

"I'm only answering your damn questions!"

"Why were you sneaking into the United States? What was your mission?"

"I was trying out my new boat. Look, I just retired from the Department of Homeland Security and you can call my buddy at DHS who is in the Coast Guard. He will verify my story."

"Mister, I don't know what you are trying to pull but there is no such thing as an area code or a Department of Homeland Security.

Your Japanese instructors didn't do a very good job briefing you. We'll wait until you are transported to shore before asking anymore questions." The two suits then left the cellblock.

CHAPTER TEN

Shortly after the suits left, I was handcuffed and led up on deck and onto an awaiting Coast Guard ship. I was then taken below and placed in the wardroom with two guards. Nothing was said for about an hour when I felt the ship slow and what sounded like a muted collision with what I suspect was the dock. The two suits entered the ward room and I was told to stand up and they blindfolded me. I was then led from the ship onto the dock and into some sort of van. Nothing was said to me except for instructions where to put my feet while walking.

The van stopped several times. Each time it stopped, I heard voices asking for identification. After about thirty minutes, we apparently arrived at our destination because I was taken out of the van and led to a building. I immediately noticed that the room was cool and smelled of mold or mildew.

My blindfold was removed and as my eyes became accustomed to the lighting, I noticed that the room was empty except for an eight foot table with one chair on one side and several on the other. There was a bare bulb light directly over the table and on the table were a number of items from my boat. They had laid out my cell phone, GPS and navigation equipment, DVD player, CDs, Ipod and navigational charts. It was just a guess but I just knew that the solitary chair was for me and this was not a quiz.

CHAPTER ELEVEN

The suits and several military officers took seats across from me and the questions started. They wanted to know what all the objects on the table were supposed to be.

"What is this?"

"My cell phone," I said.

"What is its purpose?"

"To make phone calls."

"And this?"

"That is my GPS device for finding my location at sea and to save you the trouble, that is my DVD player for watching movies. Those disks are the movies for the DVD player. That small rectangular device is my Ipod for music and also watching movies and the charts were for my shakedown cruise. I have really had enough of this. What the hell is going on here? I go for a three day sail and I'm grabbed by the United States Navy, thrown into the brig, and interrogated by the FBI, if you guys really are the FBI, accused of being a spy, dragged onto a Coast Guard ship and hauled into a room and interrogated me. I don't know what you think you are doing but September eleventh was seven years ago and you cannot treat a U.S. citizen like this anymore. Now, in 2008, there still is equal justice under law and the right to call my family and my lawyer when arrested."

"Excuse me," said the FBI suit. "What year did you say it is?"

I repeated, "2008."

The men looked at me and then left the table to another part of the room where they whispered to each other. After looking back at me numerous times, a Naval officer who I suspected was in charge because he was a captain by the eagle on his uniform, looked me straight in the eye and said, "Look, we have no time for jokes, today is the fourth of January, 1942, and you were apprehended seventy-five miles off the coast of Virginia in a Japanese boat with devices made in Japan, charts depicting the coastline of the United States and a story that no one will believe." He then slammed down a copy of the local paper with that date. "Now, let's get the truth. Who are you really and who are your handlers in the United States? Speak up or surely as there is a God in heaven you'll be dragged outside and shot as a spy."

CHAPTER TWELVE

My God! Am I dreaming? I remember falling on my boat and hitting my head on the deck. Yup, that's the answer. I'm dreaming. Maybe if I pinch myself I'll wake up. Ouch! That hurt. Then I looked up and realized they were all there staring at me.

I looked up at the men sitting across from me. "Look, this morning I was sailing off the coast of Virginia. I was on a shakedown cruise for three days and was returning to Baltimore. The date was August 3, 2008, and the items in front of you are everyday objects used for communication and steering of a ship, plane or car. The large square thing is a computer which gives access to the internet, the small rectangular object is an IPOD for my music and those disks are movies which are played on the large rectangular object. Do you have them in your time or am I on Candid Camera?"

"I don't know what you are talking about," said the

Captain, "but each and every item you have pointed out and your boat were built by the Japanese. Just in case you are not aware of your position, we have been at war with Japan since December 7, 1941, and we are losing ships every day to German submarines and warships with these kind of new inventions." The Captain then turned to the FBI agents and said, "take this spy away. Get him out of my sight."

CHAPTER THIRTEEN

As I was taken out of the room a hood was placed over my head and I was dragged over a gravel surface which I assumed was the parking lot and thrown into a vehicle I believed was some sort of a van. It felt higher off the ground than a car and I landed on the floor of the vehicle. We drove for about 30 minutes when the van suddenly stopped and I could tell that we were close to a propeller aircraft. I could hear the rotating propellers and smelled burning fuel. I was hoisted up metal stairs into the plane and strapped into a seat. My blindfold was removed and the suits strapped themselves into the adjoining seats after I was securely buckled in. One of the agents gave the command to take off and we were instantly airborne.

"This must be real. No airport in 2008 lets you take off that fast and I didn't have to take off my shoes to go through security," I said.

The FBI agents looked at me but said nothing. I was starting to realize I have got to stop my attempts at witty banter until I could get a handle on my situation. Better to keep my mouth shut until I find a lawyer.

The flight took about three hours and I was not blindfolded as we began our decent to land. I guess they blindfolded me previously because we were at a military base. I saw the Washington Monument as we approached and realized that we were flying over Washington, DC. The plane taxied past the terminal and proceeded to a building on the left. I could see several very old black cars in pristine condition with about twenty men in civilian clothes and military uniforms milling about. I was hustled off the plane and into the first black car with the two suits on either side of me. The car traveled across the Memorial Bridge and onto Constitution Avenue. Something's wrong! I know what DC looks like. The monuments are gone. There is a big empty spot where the Vietnam memorial should be. People are dressed wrong. No shorts, blue jeans, tank tops or tour buses. The buses! The buses are ancient, so are the cars. My God, it is 1942 and they do think I'm a spy.

CHAPTER FOURTEEN

We drove through DC, past the river and then kept driving for several hours once we were outside of DC. We finally drove up to a house set back from the road. The house looked like it was built in the 1930's with columns on the front porch, a wide driveway and three or four chimneys. The car drove around to the back of the house where several more suits were waiting. I was hustled down steps and into the basement of the house. My handcuffs were taken off and I was placed in a bedroom without windows. There was a bed, end tables with lamps, a writing desk and lamp and a bathroom but no phone. The door was shut and I heard the key turn in the lock. I was again their prisoner, whoever they were.

I couldn't tell what time it was but the door opened and a man in butler attire asked me to follow him upstairs. We climbed two sets of stairs and emerged in a dining room that was set for eight people. I was directed to a chair and asked if I wanted coffee or juice.

"Both, and I take the coffee black, please," I said. No reason to be rude.

The butler went over to the sideboard and filled my order. He returned with the beverages on a silver tray and took my napkin off my plate and placed it on my lap before serving my drinks.

He then asked, "how would you like your eggs? We have fish, ham, sausages and potatoes or whatever else you wish."

I asked for everything but the fish. I couldn't remember when I last ate and despite all the turmoil, I was hungry. With a nod, the butler left. The room was large. Twenty foot ceilings, plush carpet, a dinner table which could seat twenty or more and enough silver on the table to make any thief jealous. There were four other very notable objects in the room in the form of four of the biggest and meanest men I had ever seen. They were stationed at every exit and I didn't think they were there to guard the breakfast. The butler returned with my breakfast and after wishing me a good day, left the room.

As I began eating I heard voices coming down the hallway and six men enter the dining room. The butler emerged again and this time pushed a cart with various silver coffee pots, cups and saucers, orange juice decanters, and sweets. He pushed the cart around the table and served each of the eight men in turn. As they talked among themselves they occasionally looked at me but said nothing in my direction. I noticed that the suit sitting at the head of the table was the apparent leader and that a second man in a naval uniform with three stars on his epilates seemed to be his second in command. The others were dressed in typical government issued suits. The one directly across from me spoke to the other agents in a British accent. After ordering breakfast the men suddenly became quiet and the man at the head of the table addressed me directly.

"Mr. Nagol, my name is J. Edgar Hoover, and I am the Director of the FBI."

CHAPTER FIFTEEN

The man sitting at the head of the table was indeed J. Edgar Hoover. I remember seeing his picture in papers and in the movies. This was the head "G" man, the real Boss. That was when I thought to myself that I really was in a heap of trouble. Mr. Hoover then turned to the Admiral to his right and whispered something.

"Mr. Nagol," said Mr. Hoover, "let me introduce the other members at the table. Please try to refrain from any comments until I finish and explain why you are here. To my right is Admiral James Hutchinson, National Security Advisor to the President and the man who will be heading your debriefing. To his left is Professor Lawrence Gilmore from MIT, Professor Joe Mainsail from University of Chicago, Professor Edward Jones from Yale University and Mr. Gerald Hawthorn who is a Special agent with the FBI." Each nodded but did not speak.

"Mr. Nagol," said Admiral Hutchinson, "We have been going over your boat and these are items that were removed. To be honest, except for the books, we have no idea what we have. We also had experts look at the items removed from your wallet and the money taken from your clothing. My experts state that either you are an alien from outer space or a stupid spy who must have been waiving a red cape at sea wanting to be captured." I did not find that statement amusing and continued to sit quietly.

The Admiral cleared his throat and continued. "But from what I have heard and seen and with the advice of the esteemed gentlemen sitting at this table, I am leaning toward the alien theory. Can you please tell us your story again?"

I again told my story and pointed to the items that were placed on the table. I proceeded to explain the use of my computer and its capabilities, the Ipod, DVD, discs and navigational aids.

When I was done, my captors each asked questions related to their areas of expertise. The Admiral questioned my knowledge of navigation, GPS and charts. The professors wanted to know about how the computer worked and what were its capabilities. They were so fascinated about the internet that I had to repeat my story over and over since they just couldn't understand the idea of reaching anyone and everything in an instant around the world. Admiral Hutchinson and the FBI Director were focused on the books about the U.S. wars from World War II to Vietnam. It seemed that no one wanted to leave the room. We were served lunch and then dinner. That was when I reminded them that we had been going at it for over fourteen hours and I was tired. They reluctantly allowed me to go to bed.

"Strange," I said to myself. "Now there are four guards outside my door instead of one and I could hear the sounds of dogs patrolling the grounds. Do they really think I am that dangerous?"

CHAPTER SIXTEEN

I must have been really tired. I didn't remember anything after my head hit the pillow until I awoke to a light tapping on my door and the butler came in with coffee. He advised me that he had also brought a change of clothes and that breakfast would be served in forty-five minutes. I showered and shaved. It was an electric razor. I guess they didn't want me to cut my throat. Exactly forty-five minutes later there was again a knock at the door and the butler asked me to follow him. There were the customary four shadows around me and I was again led to the dining room where I ate by myself. At least you could say I was by myself if you didn't count my escorts. Around 9:00 AM the same men who interviewed me the day before arrived and after coffee they started their inquiry into my background. I was asked about my life, family and jobs I had had. After I finished, the same questions began again and again. I reminded them that I was a former police officer and this Mutt and Jeff dialogue was getting tiresome.

They broke for lunch and I ate alone. As soon as the butler cleared the dishes, the men returned and the questioning began again. The questions continued until about 10:00 PM when I was led back to my room. Before the butler closed and locked the door, I asked him for a television. He looked confused and I explained what a television. He again gave me a blank stare. I then suggested that I might be given a radio at least. The butler nodded and left.

As I lay on the bed and thought about my wife and family. Then the realization came to me. My wife had not been born yet and my parents were barely out of their teens. I was alone. I had never been born. I could be disposed of and no one would ever know.

CHAPTER SEVENTEEN

The third day began just like the rest. The butler woke me, breakfast, interrogation, lunch, more interrogation, dinner and bed. So on the fourth day, I refused to leave my room and asked that my breakfast be delivered to my room. This turned out to be an extraordinarily bad idea. My shadows simply dragged me out of my room and into the dining room where I was dumped into a chair. So I did the only thing I could think to do. I simply refused to eat or talk to my interrogators. Then, I issued my demands.

"Look guys, I have come to realize that I somehow have been transported to the past. You say August 1942. OK, I saw Washington, DC and the cars and the way people dress. No one could have put on a deception like that. But I am from the year 2008 and everything I have told you is true. My personal property, my boat and identification have undoubtedly been examined and you must know that those devices could not have been produced by any nation at this time. I am an American citizen who just retired and was taking a short boat ride in the Atlantic when I sailed into some weird fog I was knocked unconscious and ended up here. Now I find myself being held as a prisoner and suspected of being a spy. Now, we can agree at least in principal on these facts and start treating me as a citizen with rights or I'm not going to cooperate unless I talk to an attorney of my choosing. Do you understand?"

With a nod from Admiral Hutchinson, I was grabbed by my escorts and dragged back to my room.

CHAPTER EIGHTEEN

Except for the butler bringing me a change of clothes and meals, I remained in my room for what seemed like days. No one spoke to me except the butler and then it was only polite responses. Then came a knock at my door and I rose thinking it was the butler again but instead one of my guards entered and handed me a radio. Without a word, he then turned and left. I stood there for a moment in disbelief and then plugged in the radio. It took awhile for the radio to warm up but when it did Big Band music poured forth. I continued to turn the dial until I found a news program. A reporter was broadcasting on how badly the war was going in Europe and about the problems the United States was having in the Pacific. I ran to the door and pounded on it.

"Let me out! I need to talk to the Admiral Hutchinson."

No answer. Again I pounded on the door. The door

then opened and the guard told me to follow him. I was taken into the living room this time and found my interrogators waiting.

"Look, I know what is going to happen in this war and wars to come. I have books, movies and my own knowledge about how the war will be played out in both Europe and the Pacific. I don't know why I'm here but you are all fools if you don't start listening to me."

There was silence in the room and my interrogators looked at each other. Finally Admiral Hutchinson said, "You know, we had reached the same conclusion yesterday."

"Then why the hell was I confined to my room?"

"The truth is that we don't know what to do with you." the Admiral admitted, almost under his breath. "If you are what you say you are, and we are leaning in that direction, you would be just as valuable to the AXIS. If you really are a spy we couldn't really let you go, could we? Lets start all over again and look at the movies, the books and listen to what you know as it pertains to the war because, quite frankly, we are getting our butts kicked!"

CHAPTER NINETEEN

First, my being sent to my room, so to speak, must end. If I'm going to help you I must be given more freedom of the house and grounds for starters."

The FBI Special Agent and Admiral Hutchinson agreed.

"OK. I am not an expert on the Second World War but I know that after Pearl Harbor the next action in the Pacific was at the Coral Sea and Midway. I have a movie of the battle that will start on June fourth and end on June seventh. We call it the Battle of Midway. I have recordings about every major naval and surface battle of this war. Once this fight is over, it will be known as World War II. I would suggest that we focus on those two battles first before considering topic's like the Manhattan Project."

The Admiral abruptly cut in and told me that I was never to mention the Manhattan Project again and gave me a look that said I would be going back to my room permanently if I didn't comply. I told him I understood and asked if I could have the DVDs and my laptop computer. These were brought to me and I noticed that some of my DVD's were on top of a nearby phonograph. I asked why the phonograph was brought out and was told that they had tried to play the DVD's on it but without result. I blew up.

"Look you Neanderthals, these DVD's have special data on them that can only be read by a computer. The computer reads them for picture, color and sound and plays them. They are not phonograph records and I only hope you didn't destroy them. In the future, keep away from them and I will show you how to use them. Do you understand?"

All in the room shook their heads in agreement. I then opened the laptop and inserted the DVD relating to the Battle of the Coral Sea and started the movie. You would think my audience was at an opening performance minus the popcorn. Their eyes were like saucers and their lower jaws almost touched the floor. No one said a word or moved from their chairs. I even noticed that my shadows had moved closer. After the movie, the men at the table sat back in disbelief. Here was the entire battle, less the Hollywood lipstick, with dates, times and locations. The full battle plan laid in their laps. Phones were picked up and orders given. The FBI agent asked to see Director Hoover personally. I felt a tap on my shoulder and the Admiral asked me to step aside.

"While the other's are running their mouths, can I see any additional information on the Coral Sea Battle? I think I need to move on this immediately."

I located another DVD on the battle and played it.

"So," quizzed the Admiral, "The Battle of the Coral Sea begins on May fourth and lasts until May eighth?. The Battle of Midway on June fourth through the June seventh?. This is March fourth and there is little time for planning. I need to see the President."

CHAPTER TWENTY

For the next week, I showed DVDs to all who were brought to the mansion. Each day there were more Admirals, Generals and their staff than could be accommodated. There were also long hours discussing the computer and other items that the military seized from my boat. The days began at six in the morning and ran through midnight most days. The Admiral even brought in a chaplain on Sundays so I did not have to take time to go to the chapel. Then one morning I was told that I was being moved to Quantico Marine Base. The Navy was to get most of my time due to that fact that most military engagements were Navy related. I again insisted that I be given more freedom and access to base entertainment. I told them I would like to go to the bar, hang out and have some fun. I told the Admiral that some company other than his would be refreshing and having a beer would make it even better. The Admiral said he would see what he could do but my freedom was limited because were on a military base and some things just couldn't be changed. I again told them that unless my demand was met, I would not reveal the password on the computer and they could all just pound sand. The Admiral reminded me that I was an American and there was a war going on. I reminded him that although I was an American, I was being treated like a spy without any rights. I turned on my heels and went back to my room.

FBI agent George Kellan overheard all was said and walked over to the Admiral. "Are you going to give him more space?"

"Some," said the Admiral, " but only on the base. We cannot allow him to escape and tell anyone about what has happened here and what was going to happen in the future. If the media ever learned about the book the President would be impeached and we all would be hung. By the way, Mr. Hoover has selected you to oversee Mr. Nagol's security at Quantico."

The FBI agent nodded in agreement but began trying to think of a way to get the computer password in case Mr. Nagol became a liability.

CHAPTER TWENTY-ONE

The following day I was transferred from my unknown location to the Quantico Marine Base in Virginia. Transferred is really not the word for it. I was hustled into a van that resembled an armored car. As always, my shadows were with me but refused to talk to me. The trip took about seven hours and when we arrived there was a number of military police with rifles and side arms to greet me. I was transferred to a waiting staff car and then to a barracks with covered windows. It appeared that the barracks had not been used for some time bolstered by the fact that there seemed to be a problem with the heating system. I later learned the damned system was so old that it had to be coal fed by hand and impossible to regulate. There was a makeshift bedroom with a canvas type curtain that could be pulled across for privacy, a small kitchen, and leather furniture set in a circle for a living room. The bathroom section consisted of a row of toilets, urinals and about eight showers. This barrack apparently was used for about 30 servicemen. I guess in 1942, this would be considered a military mansion.

Shortly, the FBI and a bevy of high ranking military personnel began arriving followed by more furniture consisting of long tables and chairs. Several blackboards and telephones were also installed. I noted that armed military police were now stationed at the door checking identification cards. I sat in what was probably the best chair and motioned to the FBI man to speak to him.

"I thought you agreed that I would be given more freedom and access to entertainment." The FBI man laughed and told me that this barracks was just the office and that other accommodations were being prepared as we spoke. I again reminded him that I held the password to the computer and I would not cooperate unless our previous deal for more freedom was forthcoming. The Agent, whose name I learned was George, said that he would live up to the bargain.

He also introduced me to his partner, Pete Bannister, and informed me that they would be driving me every day to and from my residence and the Barracks which I decided to call this barn. Since I was still pissed at how I was being treated, I decided to ignore the pleasantries and decided to ignore their names and call them suits from now on. Later, I was taken to a large house that the suit stated was generally used for high ranking officers. The house consisted of three bedrooms, two baths, a large living room and dining room area and adjoining kitchen. However, the house was surrounded by a temporary eight foot fence that looked like it had been recently installed and it was constantly patrolled by armed soldiers with dogs.

"A prison by any other name is still a prison," I said under my breath.

CHAPTER TWENTY-TWO

On the second day I was taken to the base movie theater at nine o'clock in the morning. I thought it was an odd hour for a movie but there was popcorn, candy and coke available at the counter. When I entered the theater I saw I was the only person there except for plenty of security guards. Unfortunately, they were all armed and stationed at each exit and in strategic places around the theater. None were eating popcorn. I sat down and looked around for a cup holder and then remembered that this was 1942 and one was expected to balance their popcorn and drink on their lap. The lights went down and the show began with excerpts of the current war and how badly it was going for the British. The cartoon came on next and was followed by the feature presentation.

After the movie ended I was again placed in the staff car. Before the driver started the care, I asked if I could go to the Post Exchange to pick up a few things. There was some discussion among my handlers and then I felt about as welcome as Archie Bunker's guest from the old TV sitcom. The door of the car was slammed shut and it was clear the decision had been reached and my point of view was not the winner. I was returned to the barracks where I again showed excerpts from my movies and answered questions about what else I remembered about the war and what it was like in 2008. This went on until eleven o'clock at night when I finally asked to go to my quarters. I was driven there but this time the guards stayed outside and let me go in unaccompanied. I thought it was strange but I was so tired I did not care.

I went upstairs, stripped, took a long shower and shaved. When I was done, I put on a robe and went into the bedroom and hit the light switch. Nothing happened. I walked over to the bed and as I reached to turn on the light on the night stand, a hand suddenly touched my arm. I jumped back and heard a soft laugh that was definitely female. I realized there was a woman lying in my bed.

"Who the hell are you and what are you doing?"

She gave another low laugh and said, " I'm the entertainment you asked for or should I say company you requested. My name is, well let's say Marie, and I have special permission to visit for several hours any night you would like." With that she pulled back the covers and patted the mattress.

"I'm married and just couldn't."

"Listen, I'm here to look after you and the meter is running and it doesn't take any more dimes."

Strange as it may seem, I found myself heading for the other bedroom.

CHAPTER TWENTY- THREE

"Good morning, Mr. President," said the Admiral. "Thank you for seeing me."

The President nodded and introduced the others in the Oval Office. The Vice President, the Secretary of War, the Secretary of State, Admiral Caldwell, Admiral of the Seventh Fleet known as Seventh Fleet, Speaker of the House and Senator Whitman who was the ranking member of the Senate and Chairman of the Intelligence Committee. Of course Admiral Hutchinson knew everyone there but only he and the President knew why they were there.

"Gentlemen," began the President, "Admiral Hutchinson has something to tell you but before he does I must remind you that what is said here today is above Top Secret and does not go outside of this office without my express approval."

All nodded in agreement.

"Now, Admiral Hutchinson is going to tell you the most incredible story you have ever heard. It is the king of all science fiction stories that, if you heard it from anyone else, the men in white jackets would be taking you away. But, all you will hear today is true. I repeat, all you will hear is true. Admiral, proceed."

For the next hour the Admiral told the whole story of Mr. Nagol's remarkable travel from the year 2008 back to 1942 and his amazing ship and gadgets that were recovered by the Navy. All in attendance listened quietly and asked no questions. When Admiral Hutchinson finished, there was silence in the room.

"Gentlemen, do you have anything to say?"

Admiral Caldwell was the first to speak. "If I had not been in the Oval Office and not known Admiral Hutchinson since my academy days, I would think you all were ready for a padded cell. Is this a joke or are you really serious? Are you telling me that you have the complete war plans of the Axis powers and film footage of every battle to come and the actual outcome of the war?"

"That is exactly what I am saying," said the President.

Admiral Hutchinson cut in saying that the next battle with the Japanese will occur on the fourth of May in the Coral Sea and there was very little time to arrange a surprise for the enemy if the devices, movies and books were to be believed. "If the Japanese can establish bases there and place long range bombers, we might as well go to Australia and wait for the end of the Pacific war."

"Gentlemen," said the President, please convene and discuss this matter. You also may want to meet Mr. Nagol and see what movie footage he has. We will meet Friday at 10:00 AM and I want a battle plan to counter the Japanese by then. Thank you gentlemen."

As they filed out of the Oval Office, Admiral Hutchinson asked President Roosevelt for a few minutes.

"Mr. President, I have two issues. I must tell you that in addition to the information on upcoming battles, the information also gives the exact date and time of your death. Mr. President, you will not survive this war."

"Well then" said the President, "after telling me the date and time I order you to delete that information. Only you and I will know. Now what is the second issue?"

"Mr. President, we also found a book in Mr. Nagol's belongings that was published in the year 2000. It shows the actual messages from our Allies and that you and select members of your Cabinet knew of the approaching Japanese fleet six days before the bombing of Pearl Harbor. It proves that you allowed the attack in order to get the United States into this war. What should I do with the book?"

After some thought the President asked, "Who else knows about the book?"

"Only the FBI, myself and Mr. Nagol," said Admiral Hutchinson.

"You are to destroy the book," said the President. "If this information was ever revealed the House would impeach me and I would be found guilty by the Senate. The United States leadership would be in disarray and we could well be forced to abandon our Allies after the pacifists take over the government. I am giving you a direct order as your Commander-in-Chief. If anyone even mentions the book, I want him shipped to the Aleutians. Is that clear?"

"Perfectly, Mr. President. But how about Mr. Nagol? We cannot hope to keep him locked up indefinitely."

"As you have said Admiral, he has not even been born yet. Who would miss him?"

CHAPTER TWENTY-FOUR

The following Friday another meeting was held with the President. All present had seen the DVD on the Coral Sea battle and were amazed at the technology. However, it was clear that each was not completely sure that the evidence was not a Japanese trick.

"Gentlemen," said the President, "do we believe what we have seen and deploy whatever naval forces we have or punt? Admiral Hutchinson, I understand that if we keep allowing the Japanese to consolidate their gains in the Pacific we will eventually not have enough naval forces to keep them from gaining a solid foothold in the entire South Pacific and threaten Australia. We do have the Japanese battle plan laid before us and I think it is genuine. If we can stop or severely damage the Japanese fleet we may push them back months and allow our forces to regroup. I don't believe we have a choice. Admiral Caldwell, deploy your forces to the Coral Sea and may God have mercy on our sailors."

CHAPTER TWENTY-FIVE

On the ninth of May, 1942, I was back in the barracks at the Norfolk Naval Base when FBI Agent Kellan entered the room along with Admiral Hutchinson.

"Mr. Nagol," said the Admiral. " Everything that was displayed on your computer device was one hundred percent correct. We have given the Japanese a bloody nose and have kept them from attacking Port Moresby. Unfortunately, we lost the carrier Lexington but we were able to sink the Japanese carrier Shokaku."

"I don't understand," I said. " You knew where the Japanese fleet was located and their disposition. How could we lose the Lexington?"

"War is war," said the Admiral. "Even with the best intelligence we still lose men and ships in any battle. The main thing is that we know that your information was correct and the President has ordered all U.S. naval forces to Midway. A victory there will change the course of the Pacific war. If we follow the scenario that is outlined in your computer we can't lose. The Battle of Midway is twenty-six days away and we are deploying everything we have including all three American carriers in the Pacific. You have done something extraordinary and should be proud of yourself. I think that providence has done something extraordinary."

"As for me, I only want you to show me the front gate of this prison and let me go."

Admiral Hutchinson thought for a moment and said," I'll work on it and I guess you have earned another evening with your female friend. Enjoy."

I started to say that won't be necessary but both the Admiral and Agent Kellen had already left the room.

Later that evening as my U.S. Navy and the Japanese could lose the exact number of ships detailed in the history books. I kept thinking that it didn't make sense and trying to figure out what were the odds that the outcome stayed exactly the same. As I entered the house, the shadows remained outside and the girl was waiting for me in the dining room. She was dressed in a blue evening dress and the table was set with fine china and I noticed several bottles of wine. She helped me off with my coat and began to massage my shoulders while asking me if I had a rough day. I suddenly had a vision of the Stepford Wives but I was the one that was attached to the puppet strings. The dinner was wonderful and I drank too much. I guess it was the first time that I could start to forget my problems and the life I used to have.

After dinner she told me I needed to relax. She took

my hand and led me to the bathroom where she had drawn a hot bath. She told me to get in and soak. I tried to resist but the wine and her gentle touch won me over. I couldn't completely forget Pat but thought I was trapped in this time without her and no way home. It was just then that I realized that this was the only time that I was permitted to be without my shadows and maybe a chance to turn this situation to my favor and escape. I toweled myself off before heading to the bedroom.

CHAPTER TWENTY-SIX

When I awoke the next morning there was no trace of the girl. I thought it was funny that I didn't know her name other than the obviously fake Marie. Maybe next time I would ask her for her real name. As I walked into the barracks I found a large number of high ranking naval officers in the main viewing room. Admiral Hutchinson rose from the conference table and motioned to the officers while informing me that they were preparing for the naval battle at Midway based on the information I had given them. I was introduced as a private consultant to the group and no mention was to be made as to the origin of the information to be given. All those assembled needed to know was that naval intelligence had received information concerning the Japanese battle plan and the group meeting was to finalize the American and Allied battle plan.

I quietly took my place at the back of the room.

Admiral Hutchinson then proceeded to conduct a comprehensive overview of the battle plan being careful not to identify the source of the intelligence. There were many questions from senior officers. Most commented that the plan was placing the Navy's eggs in one basket. If the battle was lost, Hawaii and the entire west coast of the United States would be wide open to invasion. Admiral Hutchinson stated he was aware of their concerns and that we had only two fully operational carriers since the USS Yorktown had been severely damaged during the Battle of the Coral Sea but would again be operational for the battle.

Sitting there I was suddenly overcome with pride in the men seated in this room. Many would be in harms way in a few days and all would lose many friends. I bit my tongue wanting to tell them how the intelligence was obtained and to assure them that they would win the battle and cripple the Japanese fleet for the rest of the war. I thought if only I could share the knowledge and where it came from, it would give some comfort in the days ahead. The meeting ended and the officers began filing out shaking hands and slapping each other on the back. It was a gesture that said they somehow knew that they each would probably not see each other again. I found myself waving good-bye.

CHAPTER TWENTY-SEVEN

Various naval officers came and went for the next three weeks. Occasionally there were officers from allied countries and a few Army brass but this was a Navy operation. I had suggested that we move the command post closer to the West coast figuring that I might have a better chance to escape but was rebuffed and told that my knowledge and the devices made me the most valuable man in the United States and the Norfolk Naval Base was more secure.

I continued to help with details of the coming battle by using my computer which, at this point, was stored in a safe and guarded by military police both inside and outside of the building. From the number of high ranking military personnel coming and going, the rest of the base must have thought the government transferred Fort Knox here and the Navy was guarding the gold. However ,the stream of officers slowed as fourth of June approached. Admiral Hutchinson paced the room most of the time and manned the telephones. He again viewed the movies on the Midway battle as if he was sure he had forgotten something. I guess all commanders have the same thought prior to a battle.

On the morning of June 4, 1942, my shadows arrived early. The Admiral and his staff apparently had been up all night based on their overgrown five o'clock shadows and the amount of empty paper coffee cups on the table. I was acknowledged but it appeared that I was there just to be there. The phones were ringing off their hooks and the Admiral was in constant contact with the President. The first reports that came in involved Japanese fighter aircraft which attacked Midway's runway and island oil tanks. More reports came in that the Japanese fleet was located and that American fleet aircraft had started the attack.

Reports continued to come in during the day until the report saying that three Japanese fleet carriers had been sunk and that a fourth was being attacked. Cheers went up until we heard the reports that the Yorktown had been sunk. Admiral Hutchinson turned to me explaining that we only had two carriers left. The Japanese still had one carrier and a large fleet that could still accomplish their task of seizing Midway. I reminded him that history said that the fourth carrier would be sunk and the battle would be a complete American victory leading to the eventual defeat of Japan. I asked him if he really believed in the computer models and books that had, until then, given a play by play description of each battle and the exact outcome.

"Why?" I said. "Was there any anxiety over the battle?"

The Admiral 's face reddened and he said, " War can change."

"No," I said. "I believe that history does not change. It seems to be set."

With that the Admiral had my shadows escort me back to my house. I was pissed, but I again realized that history was as it should be.

There were no surprises. The dead were dead, ships that were supposed to sink in battle were sunk, planes were destroyed and the President would die before the war was over.

I kept wondering why they still needed me. The answer was that I was giving them the motive and ideas about what was going to happen but the outcome was never in doubt. I decided to give the Admiral the password for the computer and walk away tomorrow.

CHAPTER TWENTY-EIGHT

I arrived early the next morning and approached the Admiral who, along with his staff, was still basking in the Midway triumph. I explained my concerns and the reason why my continued work with him was unnecessary. I handed him the computer password and assured him that I could train a yeoman to do my job. The Admiral didn't talk for a long time.

"Mr. Nagol," said the Admiral, "I need to explain something to you. I should have talked to you sooner. You have a unique status here. Not only have you the knowledge of history and the devices to bring history to life but you also have knowledge of future events that are not on film or in your books. You have knowledge of future wars and other events that are extremely valuable to this nation. You know who will be the next President, what nations will fall, what to buy in the stock market, what songs will be hits, even who will be the future leaders in the military. Also, you have read the book."

"What book are you talking about?" I asked.

"The book that gives information about this nation allowing the attack on Pearl Harbor. It is true that our allies were giving us timely information about the location of the Japanese fleet six days prior to the attack. The President was aware of these dispatches, even the fact that one of our own submarines was tracking them. We needed as a nation to allow the attack so that the United States could enter the war. Our think tanks believe that Pearl Harbor's shallow harbor would keep the carrier ships from being sunk. Why do you think the carriers were not in the harbor when the attack occurred? What I mean is that I agree with you. I don't know if your information just tells us where to be and what forces to commit and that the outcome is cut in stone or we would have done the same thing without you but I cannot take the chance. You are the single most important man in the world at this point in time. You are also the most dangerous man alive. That is why you cannot ever be allowed out of our custody."

CHAPTER TWENTY-NINE

I went back to my house that evening with the same cloud over my head. I kept thinking about the old adage, which came first, the chicken or the egg?. Was the information in the DVDs and books the chicken or the egg? Was my information the cause of history or was history already set and the I just happen to have a recording of what was going to be no matter what. My head was spinning and I made a decision not to help anymore.

"Let history make history!" I said to myself. I would do a Pontius Pilate and wash my hands of this whole business.

The next morning the girl was in the kitchen fixing my breakfast and turned to ask me why I was still in my pajamas. I turned and told my shadows that I wouldn't be going with them. My shadows asked if I was ill but I just turned and went back to my bedroom and shut the door. I must have really confused them because an hour later there was a knock at my door and a man entered saying he was a naval doctor who had been called because my shadows thought I was sick. I told the doctor that I was fine. He insisted that he had orders from the Admiral to check me out and he began taking my pulse and temperature. I became angry and told the doctor that I was from the future, fed up with the past and just wanted to be alone. The doctor looked at me, put his stethoscope in his bag and left without another word.

"I told him," I said to myself.

Half an hour later my shadows entered my room with another doctor who told me he was a psychiatrist. He said that the first doctor told him I was delusional. He extracted a syringe from his bag and began to fill it from a small vial full of a dark yellow liquid. He then instructed my shadows to hold me so he could inject me. I yelled for him to call the Admiral but the good doctor began to swab my arm with alcohol. Just then the Admiral entered the room and asked what was going on. He and his aide looked strange since they were both dressed in exercise clothes and carrying a soccer ball.

The doctor informed the Admiral that he was about to give me a shot to calm me down. The Admiral asked me if I was ill I told him I was not but had decided not to work with him anymore and I was not going to hide the truth any longer. The Admiral dismissed the good doctor with instructions not to make any record of his visit and not to say anything to anyone. The doctor nodded and left. The Admiral then turned to me and asked why I was being so stubborn. I told him that I was fed up with the current arrangements of my custody and that I wanted out.

The Admiral thought a minute and said, "You will be at the Barracks tomorrow at eight in the morning sharp or I will place you in a cell, lock the door, and let you rot. Do I make myself clear?"

It didn't take me but a nano second to agree and the Admiral turned to leave.

"That soccer ball your aide is carrying is the answer to the explosive pattern for the nuclear device they are building at Los Alamos. You know, the one they call the Manhattan Project." Then I shut the door.

CHAPTER THIRTY

Good morning, Mr. President, " said Admiral Hutchinson.

"Thank you for coming Admiral," said the President. " I would like to introduce you to Dr. Robert Oppenheimer and General Grove who have just flown in from Los Alamos. They were astonished by your message about the triggering device for the atomic bomb. Your thought about using the soccer ball pattern is exactly the answer they were looking for. They want to know where the idea came from."

"Yes," said Dr. Oppenheimer. "Our scientists have been working on this problem for months and we have already had one fatality trying to find out the answer."

"Before you answer Admiral," said the President," I believe that you should decide what information, if any, you wish to divulge about your prisoner."

For the next hour Admiral Hutchinson gave an

overview of what transpired at the Barracks, the DVDs, books and other devices that were seized from the boat. The identity of the man seized on the boat was not divulged. When Admiral Hutchinson was finished he noted that Dr. Oppenheimer and General Grove looked at him like deer in headlights.

"Mr. President, are you pulling our legs?"

"No General. Every thing you have heard is true. In fact, our source can probably give you even more information about the Manhattan Project that just might accelerate the completion of the bomb."

"Mr. President," said General Grover, "in view of this information, your friend might very well be the most dangerous man in the world and a most serious threat to national security. If he were to be captured by the AXIS powers we would surely lose this war. I suggest that this person be sent to Los Alamos immediately for both his and this nation's safety."

"I'm sorry but that that would be impossible," said the Admiral. "I have to think of the big picture and not the lone project at Los Alamos."

"Let's compromise," said the President. "Admiral, you will double security at Quantico and General Grover will have whatever access to the information that he needs. Any conflict will be resolved by me. Any questions?"

As all were leaving, Dr. Oppenheimer turned to Admiral Hutchinson and said, " What is a laptop computer?"

CHAPTER THIRTY-ONE

How are you feeling today?" asked Admiral Hutchinson.

"Fine." I replied sarcastically. "Couldn't be happier to be working with you again."

The Admiral's eyes narrowed but replied "I met with Dr. Oppenheimer and General Grover at the White House yesterday. Both were very interested in you and wanted me to tell you that your soccer ball idea worked. You should be very proud of yourself."

"How much did you tell them?"

"Enough to let them know what level and quality of information you possess."

"I wish you had told me about your meeting in advance. I would have told you that there is a spy at Los Alamos. I'm not sure exactly who but I think the name is in my DVDs or books. I know that the Manhattan Project information is being given to the Russians as we speak and the Russians are still friends with the Germans. Russia will explode their own atomic bomb in 1948 with the information they are receiving right now. Damn! If I didn't know what was going to happen in the future I'd be suggesting that you tell everyone you know to start building a bomb shelter."

CHAPTER THIRTY-TWO

Around midnight on June 13, 1942, a German submarine surfaced off the coast of Long Island under the cover of heavy fog. The long voyage from Germany was carried out without contact with any surface ship and for the sole purpose of landing secret agents sent to capture William Nagol. Although the spy at Los Alamos was giving information to Russia, he was also doubling his profits by giving the same information to German intelligence. German intelligence had decided that Mr. Nagol was a primary target. They had also sent a second team by submarine to Florida to increase their chances of success. The German agents were told that their mission was to sabotage the electrical grid of the United States but the true mission was known only to their mission commander.

The four German agents boarded an inflatable raft and pushed off towards the Long Island shore. After making land, the agents buried their German uniforms and explosives and made their way along the beach. However, as they left the beach they were found by Coast Guard security patrolling the shoreline. Although the four gave satisfactory answers and were allowed to proceed, the guards reported the encounter to their superiors. A general search was ordered which resulted in the discovery of the buried German uniforms and explosives. An alert was sent out. The FBI eventually captured the agents but the real reason for their mission was never discovered. The second group, which landed in Florida, was not captured. They too made landing by U-Boat but were already dressed in American clothing. German Intelligence had already been tipped off about the problems in New Jersey.

The two agents that landed in Florida were trained by Abwehr. Abwehr was the name for the German intelligence division in charge of espionage. One agent was twenty-three year old Albrecht Reichman. Since the age of five, He had been raised by his maternal grandmother after his parents were killed in an auto accident. Although not pro-Nazi, his grandmother hated the way Germany had been treated after World War I.

Albrecht was a trouble maker while growing up in New York. He had dropped out of high school in his junior year and took up with street gangs which ended up with him being sent to a juvenile detention facility three different times. That was where he learned to be a bully and was often abused by the staff. After he turned sixteen, he was again arrested for a fight in which he had broken a man's jaw. The guy had accidentally bumped into Albrecht in a bar. After that arrest, his grandmother sent him to Germany to live with her relatives in an attempt to straighten him out.

After arriving in Germany, Albrecht joined the Heer as the German Army was known, where he excelled and moved quickly up the ranks to Scharfuhrer, or sergeant. It was there that he was recruited by the Abwehr and trained as a spy.

The second agent was Ralf Weiss. Unlike Albrecht, he was raised by his patriotic German parents who arrived in the United States as refugees after WWI when Ralf was only three years old. Ralf's father worked at small time jobs, drank to excess and frequently abused Ralf and his mother. He would rant about the inequality of the American system and glorify the Fatherland. At fifteen, Ralf got into a fight at school and was expelled after the other student suffered a coma when Ralf hit him with a pipe. Ralf was arrested and charged as an adult and was sentenced to three years imprisonment.

While in jail he was frequently placed in solitary for fighting and disrespect to his guards. After one episode when he struck a guard, he was severely beaten by other guards. The beating left him with a scarred face and required a three month stay in the prison hospital. It was there that he befriended a German born prisoner named Freddy who told him of the Fatherland. Freddy taught Ralf how to play chess and encouraged him to frequent the prison library and avail himself of the recreational facilities at the prison. Ralf's demeanor improved and after another year, Ralf was paroled. However, unable to find a job, Ralf was again involved in a fight and this time killed the other man. Fearing prison, Ralf got a job on a tramp steamer which took him to Germany. He joined the army and rose to the rank of Rottenfuhrer or corporal. Based on his background, the Abwehr recruited him in 1937 as a spy.

Both Albrecht and Ralf were in training when they were abruptly summoned to the Director's office. There they were met by none other than Wilhelm Canaris, the head of Abwehr. Both were told that their training was to be interrupted for a special mission. They were told that there was a U-Boat waiting for them to transport them to the United States to a point south of Miami, Florida. From there they would make their way north to Culpeper, Virginia. They were given the name of a sympathetic German American that would house them until they received further instructions. No further information was given about their assignment. Money, identification and clothing were to be provided. Under no circumstance were they to identify their true names to the U-Boat commander, crew or to the contact in the United States. They were to leave immediately.

"One last thing," said Canaris, "Once you both receive your final instructions in America you cannot be captured. Let me be clear, if one or both of you is about to be captured it will be your duty to either take the cyanide pill that will be provided or to shoot each other. The Americans cannot, I repeat, cannot know the real purpose of your assignment." Both Ralf and Albrecht nodded.

As they walked down the hallway, Ralf looked at Albrecht and said, " Do you have the feeling that this is a suicide mission?"

Albrecht said nothing but from the look on his face, Ralf knew he agreed with him.

CHAPTER THIRTY-THREE

It was July 20, 1942 and the German U-boat designated as U-285, was sitting off the coast of Miami, Florida.

"Captain, we have reached our objective," said the First Officer.

"Good, said the Captain. Sound, anything in the area?"

"No Captain, nothing in range."

The Captain gave the order to raise the periscope. A quick scan of the area confirmed the soundman's words.

"Good, no moon and overcast. Surface!"

As if listening to her human master, U-285 surfaced as if of its own accord.

"Open the hatch and load the raft. Come on, we cannot stay surfaced for long," ordered the Captain.

The crew responded smartly and soon the agents were in the raft and paddling away from the submarine.

The Captain took one last look from the periscope before the water

overtook the submarine.

"Submerge! Radio, report that we have completed our mission. Now, let's go hunting," said the Captain as he rubbed his hands together.

The German agents landed on American soil and quickly punctured the raft; watching while it sank beneath the waves. After walking about a mile the agents spotted a small out of the way bar where they ordered beers and food. When done with their meal, the called a cab which took them to the bus station where they bought tickets for Columbia, South Carolina. They would continue to buy bus tickets for cities while traveling up U.S. Route 301 until reaching Culpeper, Virginia. They believed that anyone tracking them would be delayed thinking that they were still in various cities. It was easy for both agents since each had grown up in the United States and had left for Germany before WWII began. And anyway, they were flush with money and their cover story as rich sons from New York was easily accepted by those with little money and less food due to shortages imposed by the government's war efforts.

The agents were instructed to use only buses for travel, not to wait too long at bus stops but rather to take any bus traveling north, even if it was not in a direct route to their final destination. Each carried a small handgun, a Colt, and one other very important item, both in case of capture, a cyanide pill. However, as they approached

Virginia, the two agents switched from buses and began hitchhiking and using back roads because government security on the public transportation increased as they got closer to Washington, DC. The agents also changed their identity papers each day so that no trace through motels could alert the authorities. A few days later, the two agents arrived at the small town of Culpeper, Virginia where they were hidden by a sympathetic German. There they were given a coded message telling them to stay under cover until they were contacted again.

CHAPTER THIRTY-FOUR

Returning to my residence at Quantico, the girl was there again and busy in the kitchen. I grabbed her around the waist and without a word carried her to the bedroom. For the next few hours I was not exactly gentle. My mind was clouded by the threats made by Admiral Hutchinson and my own needs. I guess I fell asleep because the next thing I knew is that is was dawn. The girl was still sleeping there asleep. This surprised me . Generally she disappeared as quietly as she appeared. I studied her for awhile noting her breasts peeking out of my shirt she had borrowed and how they rose with each breath. I placed my hand on her breast closet to me. She gave a soft moan and uttered Agent Kellen's name.

Shocked, I went to the bathroom and turned on the shower. I made up my mind this was the last straw. I was determined not to see the girl again. What an idiot I had been. I should have realized that the girl was a spy for either Admiral Hutchinson or the FBI and I bet she made sure that everything I said or did was immediately reported to her boss. Then I noticed her standing behind me. As I turned, I did something I had never done to a woman before; I slapped her on the face.

"Bitch! You should be more careful about talking in your sleep. You are nothing more than a prostitute. Get out!."

A tear suddenly appeared on her face.

"Stop it! Your tricks are not going to work on me anymore."

Without a sound she placed her finger to her lips and pointed to the medicine cabinet. As I examined the medicine cabinet carefully, I saw a small wire. The damn room was bugged. I quickly dressed and headed to the Barracks with my shadows in tow. Later, I returned to my residence and was hoping to see the girl but found only a note alongside my dinner plate. The note instructed me to check the icebox for my dinner and had the words 'Thanks for last night' written across it.

"What a crock." I thought. She was probably in bed with the Admiral or Agent Kellen right now telling him everything. I am sure both were having a good laugh. Still, I couldn't help but think that the tear was real. Tearing up the note, I told myself that any information that passed my lips from that point on would be minimal. I knew that I needed to escape and if the girl appeared again, I would either give her an experience that would probably get the good doctor to visit me again or try to see if I could use her to escape.

CHAPTER THIRTY-FIVE

The next morning I was told by my shadows that I was to expect visitors. About nine o'clock in the morning there was a knock at the barracks door. General Grover and Dr. Oppenheimer entered. All of my devices were arranged on the main table and I was advised by Admiral Hutchinson to explain and demonstrate the use of each. I entered the password in the laptop and proceeded to explain the function of my computer and the other devices, DVDs and books.

Dr. Oppenheimer was like a kid in a candy store; asking question after question. He was especially focused on the math function and memory of the laptop. I then placed a DVD in the computer, dimmed the lights and watched in fascination the reactions of my guests during the two-hour presentation. The only thing missing was the popcorn. I later explained that the DVD information about the war was factual and that these are the events as they would happen in the future. You can imagine his shock when he actually saw the atomic bomb explosion in Nevada. He was stunned by its power. I believe that this was the reason that later he would protest the use of the bomb. I could tell by the look Dr. Oppenheimer gave me as he left that he knew that he had witnessed the future and he did not like what he saw. I never saw him again.

CHAPTER THIRTY-SIX

The two German agents waited two days until a phone call alerted them by special code that they would be met that evening by their German contact with operational plans. At about nine o'clock at night a car turned into the driveway of the Culpeper hideout. Out stepped one of the highest ranking German moles currently working in the United States. His identity was FBI agent George Kellan and he had been sending secret dispatches to German Intelligence for the past four months.

Agent Kellen was recruited by the Abwher in 1940, prior to the United States entering the war. It wasn't difficult. Agent Kellen had been eating lunch at a local restaurant when he was approached by a German Abwher agent. The agent handed Kellen photos that had been taken the night before. Agent Kellen's secret was there in black and white. The man from Abwher told Agent Kellen that unless he cooperated, the photos would be sent to the FBI. Agent Kellen stared at the photos, looking first at own face and then at the face of his male lover. He knew that the photos meant the loss of his family and his career and agreed to work for the Abwher. Agent Kellen immediately began to provide documents to his German handler.

When Mr. Nagol was found, Agent Kellen was assigned to interview him by his superiors and had been dumbfounded by what he heard. He immediately contacted his German handler who at first thought the information was a fake intended to lead to his capture. However, after Agent Kellan gave him sketches of the seized equipment and transcripts of the interrogation of Mr. Nagol, his handler immediately contacted German Intelligence who ordered that Agent Kellen find a way to stay on the Nagol investigation. It was everything the Abwher could hope for when Agent Kellen was assigned to be Nagol's shadow. Agent Kellen's weekly report was so classified that a copy was sent to Hitler himself.

The handler had told Agent Kellen that the Germans must have the devices and Mr. Nagol. The intelligence in the report was not sufficient. The German agents contacted Agent Kellen and he laid out the mission to kidnap Nagol and retrieve all of the devices from Quantico. The mission required all three to gain entry onto the Quantico Marine Base, kidnap or kill William Nagol and seize any devices available at the Barracks. On August 3, 1942, in the early morning, Agent Kellen, after disposing of the other FBI agent, was to drive onto the Quantico base with the two German agents disguised as naval officers.

Agent Kellen had become friends with the Marine guards he saw every morning as he entered the base. He had regularly brought coffee and donuts in order to befriend them. This now enabled him to pass through the gate without showing identity papers or search of his government car. Since he worked with Admiral Hutchinson and regularly brought naval officers through the main entrance, his mere mention that the men in the car were naval officers was sufficient for the guards to pass them through without inspection. Agent Kellen would use the guard's misplaced trust not only to enter the base but to also sneak William Nagol and the secret devices off the base without interference.

The plan called for the two German agents to be let off on Neville Road within the Quantico base. After the two German agents exited the staff car they would carry explosives and weapons in naval flight bags and make their way to the back of the Barracks and wait for Agent Kellen to pick up William Nagol and drive him to the Barracks. Upon arrival at the Barracks, Agent Kellen would kill the guard at the main gate and enter the Barracks killing anyone else who might be present. This would be the signal for the other German agents to move forward and kill any other military personnel.

To accomplish this part of the mission, William Nagol would be sedated after being picked up by Agent Kellen and put in the front seat of the staff car. This would make it look like there were two people in the staff car as it approached the barracks. This was necessary so the sentry guard would not think something was amiss as two FBI agents were required to transport Mr. Nagol. After arriving at the Barracks and disposing of the guards, Mr. Nagol would be transferred to the back seat of the car so that one agent would be free to use whatever force was needed while escaping and freeing one German agent to cover the rear of the car and watch their prisoner.

Agent Kellen again went over the order of importance of the devices which were to be seized in case they were discovered and a hasty retreat was required. The computer and the DVDs were the first priority and Agent Kellen had made drawings of each so the agents could quickly identify them. Once all was in place, Agent Kellen would then drive the car off the base. It was hoped that the quick pace of the mission would allow the car to pass the main gate before any alarm was issued. The car would be ditched a short distance away from Quantico where a second car was parked and the agents would travel to another safe house on the Eastern Shore of Maryland to await a submarine to transport them back to Germany. The plan was to be put into operation the next morning as word had come that Mr. Nagol was to be moved to Los Alamos within the next four days.

CHAPTER THIRTY-SEVEN

The following morning Agent Kellen arrived early at the Culpeper, Virginia safe house. He brought American naval officer uniforms, weapons and identity cards for the two German Agents. In the trunk was the body of FBI Agent Bannister who Agent Kellen had killed earlier when he had picked him up for the routine morning ride to work. It was well planned. After arriving at Agent Bannister's house, Agent Kellen had told Agent Bannister that he had a slow leak in the left front tire and needed help changing the tire. As Agent Bannister opened the trunk and leaned in to remove the spare tire a short thrust with a thin blade into the back of Agent Bannister's neck severed the spinal cord which immediately immobilized and mortally wounded him and Agent Kellen had watched him slowly die.

If Kellen had any remorse, he didn't show it. The only thing on his mind was the mission. As the agents dressed, they went over the Quantico maps and rehearsed their roles. At four in the morning on August 3, 1942, Agent Kellen took the drivers seat and the two German agents occupied the rear seat. Their loaded weapons were placed on the rear floor covered by a blanket in case they were needed in a hurry. Agent Kellen also carried a syringe to incapacitate William Nagol after he was picked up at his residence.

Leaving the safe house, the car turned East on Virginia Route Three and proceeded North on Route One towards the town of Quantico. Few words were spoken and Agent Kellen pulled over at the town of Quantico to pick up coffee and donuts for the Marine Guards at the main gate. Feeling energized, Agent Kellen ordered two dozen donuts and four cups of coffee feeling that the surprise would assure him entry without inspection of the two agents in the rear seat.

Driving up to the main gate at Quantico, Agent Kellen noticed additional guards admitting cars. Unknown to him, Admiral Hutchinson had implemented additional security as advised by the President. Agent Kellen continued towards the gate fearing that if he turned around he would bring suspicion on himself. As he stopped at the gate a guard he knew as Henry approached the car with a flashlight. Henry recognized Kellen as George the FBI Agent and relaxed. Agent Kellen thrust the donuts and coffee at the guard requiring him to place his flashlight on his belt and grab the offering. Agent Kellen then identified the two naval officers in the rear seat. They showed their identity cards but the guard was unable to get a close look without his flashlight. The guard thanked Agent Kellen and told him to proceed.

"That was easy," said one agent from the back seat which elicited a laugh from everyone in the car.

CHAPTER THIRTY-EIGHT

Unknown to Agent Kellen, a naval lieutenant was at the guard shack when the car was allowed to enter the Marine base. He immediately inquired of Lance Corporal Henry why he had failed to obey his orders to search all vehicles entering the base.

"Gee, Lieutenant, that was FBI agent George. He enters every day and works with Admiral Hutchinson. He often brings in military officers for meetings with the Admiral and escorts the prisoner at the Residence to the Barracks. There was no reason to search his car."

"I don't care," said the Lieutenant. "I'm not getting slapped with an Article 15 disciplinary action or worse because you failed to comply with the base Commander's orders. Get me the Barracks on the phone."

The phone rang at the Barracks. " Good morning, Admiral Hutchinson's office,"

"Sir, this is Lieutenant Anderson at the main gate.

FBI agent George, don't know his last name, was just admitted with two naval officers and he went through without having his car searched. I know he works with Admiral Hutchinson but the Base Commander gave specific orders that all vehicles be searched. I would appreciate if he could accommodate the guards at the main gate."

"Just a minute," said Commander Edwards. "Admiral, sorry to bother you but I have Lt. Anderson on the phone complaining about Agent George's entry this morning with two naval officers and not having his car searched. I think he means Agent George Kellen."

"What naval officers? I'm not expecting any visitors today. Let me have that phone. Lieutenant Anderson, this is Admiral Hutchinson, please identify the naval officers in Agent Kellen's car."

"I'm sorry Sir. The guard saw their identity cards but did not record their names."

"What did the FBI agents tell the guard?" said Admiral Hutchinson.

"There was only one FBI agent in the car Admiral, and he stated that the naval officers were here to meet with you."

"Lieutenant, this is an order. You are to seal that gate and send your men to locate Agent Kellen and escort him and whoever is in his car to my office. Do you understand?"

CHAPTER THIRTY-NINE

Commander, get me the Residence," barked Admiral Hutchinson.

"Sir, I have the guard station at the residence."

"This is Admiral Hutchinson, let me speak to Agent Kellen."

"Sorry sir." said the guard. "Agent Kellen has picked up Mr. Nagol and is on his way to the Barracks."

The Admiral slammed down the phone. He immediately picked it back up and called Base security and demanded that all available security officers search the base for Agent Kellen and arrest him on sight.

Commander Edwards turned to the Admiral. "Sir, Agent Kellen's car is pulling up as we speak."

The Admiral opened the Barrack's door and stormed out all the while barking orders that the Barrack's security guards follow him. He was hell bent on finding out what was happening. However, before he could speak he heard gunfire coming from the rear of the Barracks and he could see that several of his security guards were hit. The gunfire continued but was now aimed at the guardhouse immediately to the front of the Barracks.

The four guards returned fire but were mowed down by the unseen shooters. As Admiral Hutchinson turned in the direction of the man he knew as Agent Kellen, he saw the drawn his revolver and pointing towards him. The gun barked and Commander Edwards let out a short yell then collapsed. Agent Kellen walked towards Admiral Hutchinson and was joined by two unknown naval officers who were shouting in German. They immediately entered the Barracks and returned with a box containing the devices that had been seized from the Nagol yacht.

Agent Kellen coldly stared at the Admiral and said, "Please get in the car. You are our ticket out of here.

CHAPTER FORTY

The Admiral and one of the German agents sat in the rear seat of the car. Agent Kellen got in behind the wheel with the other German agent riding shotgun. Admiral Hutchinson noticed that William Nagol was slumped over and appeared to be asleep. The car sped away from the Barracks and headed towards the main Quantico gate. Kellen was driving faster than usual. This was noticed by the security guards and the security vehicles started to follow Kellen's car. Kellen sped up and the security vehicles started to chase the car. As Agent Kellen approached the main gate he noticed that the gate's arm was down and the security officer's had their weapons drawn. Agent Kellen increased his speed and aimed his car towards the entry side of the gate seeing that fewer security guards had positioned themselves there. At a hundred yards, the German agent sitting in the front passenger seat put his automatic revolver out of the window and opened fire which the guards returned.

It was right then that Admiral Hutchinson suddenly struck Agent Kellen on the back of the head with his fist causing him to lose control of the car. The car careened and impacted the left side of the guard shack before turning over and catching fire. The guards rushed over and began pulling William Nagol, one of the German agents and Admiral Hutchinson out of the car. After dragging the three to safety, the guards started back to the care to rescue the rest of the occupants. Before they could reach the care, the gas tank exploded killing Agent Kellen and the other German agent. Admiral Hutchinson was dazed but not seriously harmed. He saw that the devices were scattered across the street and immediately ordered them collected and secured. He then asked about the occupants in the car and was told that Mr. Nagol had been pulled from the car but Agent Kellen and the other two officers were dead.

"How is Mr. Nagol?" demanded Admiral Hutchinson. "Is he alive?"

"He has a gun shot to the chest and also suffered severe injuries in the accident," said the corpsman.

"Get him to the hospital now, do you understand me? Now!" ordered the Admiral.

Lance Corporal Henry Jacobson approached the Admiral.

"Admiral, after you left the main gate we found FBI Agent Bannister in the truck of the car. He is dead. I also have to inform you that the girl at the residence,

Marie, I think that was her name, was also found dead. She had been stabbed in the back of her neck just like Agent Bannister."

"That son of a bitch!" said the Admiral.

"I beg your pardon Sir?" said Lance Corporal Henry Jacobson.

"Agent Kellen, you son of a bitch," said Admiral Hutchinson as he walked away.

CHAPTER FORTY-ONE

William Nagol was rushed to the base hospital and taken to surgery. Surgeons were already busy with a pregnant woman giving birth in an adjacent operating room. One of the surgeons immediately entered Mr. Nagol's room and began directing staff while determining the extent of the injuries. Of greatest concern was a bullet wound to the chest and his low blood pressure. The surgeon ordered the nurse to get more blood and nurses in there fast.

Upon arrival at the hospital Admiral Hutchinson asked for an immediate update on Mr. Nagol. He was advised that the patient was in critical condition with a gunshot wound to the chest and that everything possible was being done. The Admiral asked to be notified at every one half hour increment about Mr. Nagol's condition and returned to the Barracks. Using the secure phone the Admiral called the President with the bad news. While he was on the line, several FBI agents entered with another man the Admiral knew, the Director of the FBI. Admiral Hutchinson informed the President that Director Hoover had arrived and the President asked that all other persons at the Barrack's be excused so that the three could talk in private.

The conversation centered on the fact that a FBI agent was in reality a German agent and that Germany knew about William Nagol and the top secret devices. The FBI Director ordered additional men to the base to begin an investigation and informed the President that an internal investigation was also being conducted on the background of Agent Kellen. He also informed the Admiral that the devices were to be immediately flown to Los Alamos as the Barracks was no longer considered safe. They would transfer Mr. Nagol there as soon as he could travel.

This brought an immediate objection from Admiral Hutchinson but he was cut off by the President who informed the Admiral that was an order and hung up. The Admiral gave the appropriate orders for the devices to be transferred under special guards and informed his staff that he could be found at the base hospital.

CHAPTER FORTY-TWO

Arriving at the base hospital, the Admiral was told that Mr. Nagol's condition had deteriorated, that the surgery was continuing and that his prognosis was not good. Suddenly, there was a cry from the adjacent operating room as the child came into the world. This was interrupted by a scream from Mr. Nagol's operating room and the Admiral quickly went in the room. There on the operating table was Mr. Nagol's body. It was fading and becoming transparent. Then it completely disappeared, leaving only his clothes and a bullet on the table. After the initial shock, Admiral Hutchinson ordered the operating room secured and had guards placed at the door.

CHAPTER FORTY-THREE

Are you alright Mister?"

"What? What did you say?" sputtered William Nagol.

"I said, are you alright."

"Yeah, I guess so. My head hurts though," said Nagol.

"Yeah, I would guess so seeing that there is a large gash on your forehead and you have lost a lot of blood. Luckily we spotted your boat. There is a helicopter on the way to take you to the hospital."

As my eyes cleared I saw that an IV had been inserted into my left hand and that a man was holding a bandage on my forehead. I could see that the men helping me were wearing military fatigues and I thanked them for saving me from the kidnappers.

"What kidnappers?" said the man holding the bandage to my head.

"You know, ask Admiral Hutchinson and he will fill you in," I muttered.

"Man, you must have hit your head too hard. Look, were part of the crew from the United States. Destroyer Shepherd. We saw your yacht drifting and after boarding, found you lying on the deck unconscious. I don't know who Admiral Hutchinson is but we have a copter coming and we'll transport you to a hospital," said the corpsman.

"What? What date is it?"

"August 23, 2008," said the Corpsman.

"I'm back. I am really back!" I said to myself.

CHAPTER FORTY-FOUR

The sun came in the window at the Eastern Shore Regional Hospital in Maryland.

"Honey, are you all right? Damn, I told you not to sail alone. I told you it wasn't safe," said my wife.

"Nice to see you too," I said as she leaned over and kissed me.

"I must have really cracked my head. I had the most vivid dream about my going back in time to WWII and that the Feds locked me up as a spy. I was kidnapped by German agents and shot."

"My, what an imagination," said my wife.

"But it seemed so real. There was the Barracks where I went every day and I met Dr. Oppenheimer and General Grove. There was a house and I was kept there and the girl that cooked and took care of me."

"What girl?" interjected my wife.

"I don't remember her name. Marie, I think. She was just in my dream," I offered sheepishly.

"Just wait until you get home and we will discuss your penchant for dreaming about other women!"

Then my wife kissed me again and told me how much she loved me and we were selling the boat.

"Yes,. Now I know I'm home again."

EPILOGUE

I had been home for about two weeks and my wife was out shopping when the doorbell rang. I opened the door and a man thrust an FBI badge in my face.

"Hello, my name is Agent Foster with the FBI and we need to speak to you."

I thought about slamming the door in his face but decided otherwise. Of course the large black Ford parked in front of my house with two other men inside made the choice easier.

"Come in. Can I get you something to drink?"

Agent Foster shook his head "No, I only need to talk to you. Have you ever heard of Justice Henry Jacobson?"

"Sure, he was a Congressman, Governor, Senator and sat on the Supreme Court until he retired several years ago."

"Well, he knows you and that is the reason I'm here,"

said Agent Foster. "A few days ago Justice Jacobson made a surprise visit to the FBI Director. He had an unbelievable story to tell. He related an incident back in 1942 when he was in the Marine Corps and stationed at Quantico Marine Base in Virginia. He was assigned to base security and while there he was placed on a special detail to guard a man that was supposed to be a Japanese spy although he said he was an American.

Anyway, being around this man he learned that his name was William Nagol and that he was snatched from a Japanese yacht out in the Atlantic and brought to Quantico. He also told of some devices that an Admiral Hutchinson was very interested in that were found with Mr. Nagol. He was in Mr. Nagol's house when Nagol told a Navy doctor this story about being from the future while the doctor examined Nagol. Anyway, Justice Jacobson told the Director that an FBI agent assigned to the detail was actually a German spy who, with two other German agents, kidnapped Mr. Nagol, stole several secret devices and attempted to flee Quantico. Fortunately, their car was intercepted. The German agents and the FBI spy were killed. Mr. Nagol was wounded by friendly fire during the escape attempt and was rushed to the base hospital. Justice Jacobson, a Lance Corporal was ordered to ride with the ambulance and was guarding the operating door when Nagol was pronounced dead and his body disappeared right off of the operating table."

I was able to stammer a faint "what?"

"Let me finish. There is more," said Agent Foster.

"When the body disappeared, a bullet was left on the table along with clothing. The operating room was sealed and it was later dismantled. All information on this man was classified above Top Secret and all parties involved were threatened with treason or banishment to the North Pole if they ever divulged the story. Justice Jacobson was also told later that the secret devices also disappeared at the same time as Nagol's body.

After Justice Jacobson finished his story and left, my Director asked me to look into the story."

"But why would Justice Jacobson come forward now," I asked.

"Apparently, the Judge read a story in the newspaper about a yacht being rescued by the Coast Guard and that a man named William Nagol was airlifted to an area hospital. It would seem that the Justice put two and two together and came up with you.

Anyway, I was asked by the Director to look into this and found out something interesting. It seems that you were born into a Marine family that was stationed at Quantico. Records show that at the same time the body of William Nagol disappeared a woman gave birth to a baby boy in the adjacent operating room. Her name was Wendy Nagol and she named her son was named William. That son was you and you were born on August 3, 1942, at Quantico, Virginia. The fingerprint card taken at that child's birth was located in military records at the federal repository in Suitland, Maryland and compared with your military records.

The fingerprint card taken at your birth matches

your fingerprints we have on record from your federal employment. We pulled the information in the Top Secret file and the fingerprints of the adult arrested in 1942 as a spy also match yours. It would appear that you have lived two lifetimes. You, Mr. Nagol, lived in 1942 as an adult and at that time provided intelligence that led to this country winning WWII and the development of the atomic bomb. Sir, you may have contributed more to the security of this country that any man in history. What I need from you today is for you to fill in the blanks as to how you accomplished time travel and what actually happened sixty-two years ago."

I talked with Agent Foster for the next few hours. He videotaped the entire conversation. Afterwards, he thanked me and politely but firmly reminded me that this meeting never happened and no records would ever be allowed to be published. Agent Foster then exited my life.

When I think about what happened to me 62 years ago I cannot help but reflect on the old adage about the chicken and the egg. Did I really change history or was I just repeating it? I think I have the answer. You really cannot change history or my wife's mind. Oh yes, I sold the boat.

William Logan is retired from the U.S. Navy, Washington Metropolitan Police Department and the Department of Homeland Security. He lives with his wife in Virginia.